TULSA CITY-COUNTY LIBRARY

P9-AOQ-330

FEB - - 2022

THE WORLD OF OCEAN ANIMALS
MANATEES

by Mari Schuh

pogo

Ideas for Parents and Teachers

Pogo Books let children practice reading informational text while introducing them to nonfiction features such as headings, labels, sidebars, maps, and diagrams, as well as a table of contents, glossary, and index.

Carefully leveled text with a strong photo match offers early fluent readers the support they need to succeed.

Before Reading

- "Walk" through the book and point out the various nonfiction features. Ask the student what purpose each feature serves.
- Look at the glossary together. Read and discuss the words.

Read the Book

- Have the child read the book independently.
- Invite him or her to list questions that arise from reading.

After Reading

- Discuss the child's questions. Talk about how he or she might find answers to those questions.
- Prompt the child to think more. Ask: Manatees live in warm, shallow ocean water. What other animals live in this habitat?

Pogo Books are published by Jump!
5357 Penn Avenue South
Minneapolis, MN 55419
www.jumplibrary.com

Copyright © 2022 Jump!
International copyright reserved in all countries. No part of this book may be reproduced in any form without written permission from the publisher.

Library of Congress Cataloging-in-Publication Data

Names: Schuh, Mari C., 1975- author.
Title: Manatees / by Mari Schuh.
Description: Minneapolis: Jump!, Inc., [2022]
Series: The world of ocean animals
Includes index. | Audience: Ages 7–10
Identifiers: LCCN 2020054211 (print)
LCCN 2020054212 (ebook)
ISBN 9781636900575 (hardcover)
ISBN 9781636900582 (paperback)
ISBN 9781636900599 (ebook)
Subjects: LCSH: Manatees—Juvenile literature.
Classification: LCC QL737.S63 S385 2022 (print)
LCC QL737.S63 (ebook) | DDC 599.55—dc23
LC record available at https://lccn.loc.gov/2020054211
LC ebook record available at https://lccn.loc.gov/2020054212

Editor: Jenna Gleisner
Designer: Michelle Sonnek

Photo Credits: Andrea Izzotti/Shutterstock, cover; RonMasessa/iStock, 1; imageBROKER/Alamy, 3, 19; All Canada Photos/Alamy, 4, 14-15; Natalie11345/Shutterstock, 5; 33karen33/iStock, 6-7; David Fleetham/Alamy, 8-9; Colors and shapes of underwater world/Getty, 10; Stephen Frink Collection/Alamy, 11; Aneese/iStock, 12-13; Kent Weakley/Shutterstock, 16-17; James R.D. Scott/Getty, 18; mauritius images GmbH/Alamy, 20-21; Jeff Stamer/Shutterstock, 23.

Printed in the United States of America at Corporate Graphics in North Mankato, Minnesota.

TABLE OF CONTENTS

CHAPTER 1

GENTLE AND SLOW

A manatee swims slowly in shallow water. Its skin is thick and wrinkled. It is big and round. Manatees can be 15 feet (4.6 meters) long. The heaviest can weigh around 3,500 pounds (1,600 kilograms)!

Manatees are gentle and peaceful. They do not fight. Some manatees swim alone. Others swim in pairs or small groups.

Manatees can move quickly in short bursts. But most of the time, they are slow swimmers. They move their wide tails up and down. Flippers help them **steer**. Flippers also come in handy in shallow water. How? Manatees use them to push along the ocean floor.

TAKE A LOOK!

What are a manatee's body parts called? Take a look!

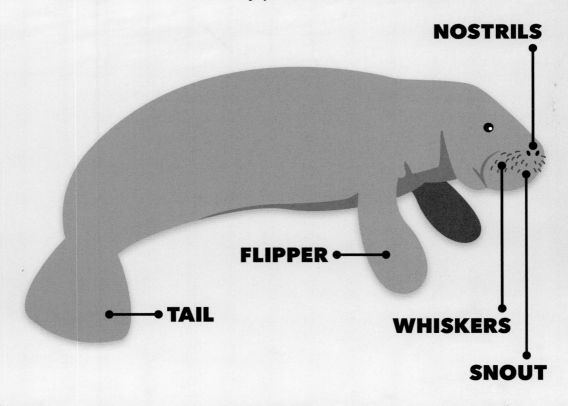

NOSTRILS

FLIPPER

TAIL

WHISKERS

SNOUT

Most marine **mammals** have layers of **blubber** to keep them warm. Manatees do not. This means they need to live in warm water. They usually swim in warm, shallow water near the **coast**. When the weather gets cold, they **migrate** to warmer water.

TAKE A LOOK!

There are three manatee **species**. The West Indian manatee is the most well-known. Take a look at where it lives!

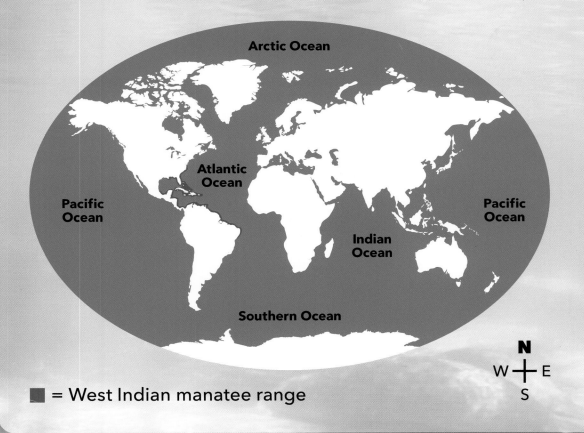

Arctic Ocean

Atlantic Ocean

Pacific Ocean

Pacific Ocean

Indian Ocean

Southern Ocean

N
W + E
S

■ = West Indian manatee range

CHAPTER 2

EATING AND RESTING

Manatees are mostly **herbivores**. They eat grasses, **algae**, and weeds that grow in the water. And they eat a lot of them! They often eat for six to eight hours a day.

They use their flippers to push food toward their mouths. Their big, **flexible** lips help them chew.

nostril

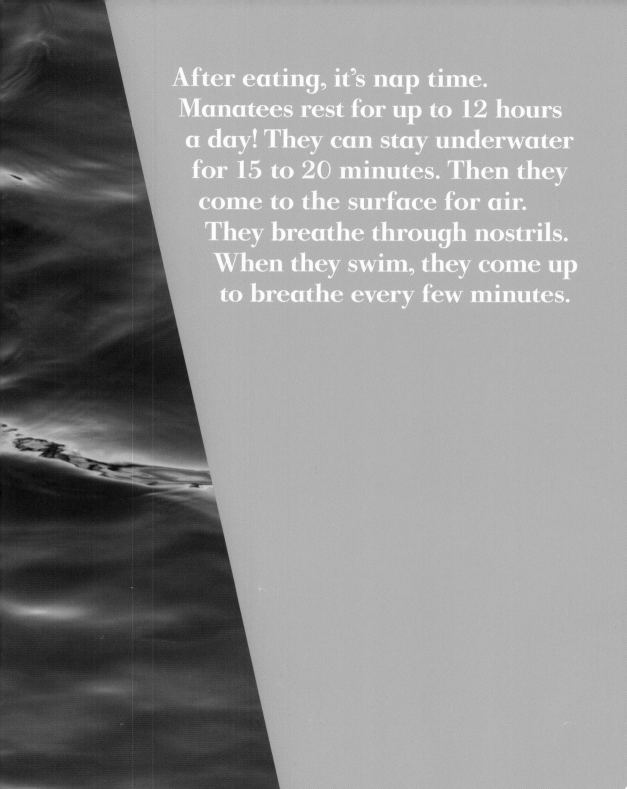

After eating, it's nap time. Manatees rest for up to 12 hours a day! They can stay underwater for 15 to 20 minutes. Then they come to the surface for air. They breathe through nostrils. When they swim, they come up to breathe every few minutes.

Algae can grow on a manatee's body. How? Manatees live in sunny areas where algae easily grow. Manatees move slowly. This gives algae time to grow. Fish eat the algae off of manatees' skin.

DID YOU KNOW?

Manatees are sometimes called sea cows. Why? They move slowly like cows. They also eat grass like cows.

Manatees are playful. They ride waves and **currents**. They also seem to play games like follow-the-leader. Moving together in one line, they all dive and move at the same time. They all come up to breathe at the same time, too.

DID YOU KNOW?

Manatees chirp and whistle. They squeak and grunt. This is how they **communicate**.

CHAPTER 3

MOTHERS AND CALVES

Manatees give birth to live young. Every few years, a female gives birth to just one **calf**. The calf is born underwater. Like its parents, it will spend its whole life underwater.

calf

A few hours after it is born, the calf drinks its mother's milk. After a few weeks, it also eats plants. The calf continues to drink its mother's milk for one to two years as it grows.

Mothers teach their calves many things. They show them good paths to travel. Calves learn where to eat and rest. They learn where to find warm water to live.

DID YOU KNOW?

Manatees do not have any **predators**. But boat propellers, hunting, and **pollution** harm them. Manatees need clean water to be healthy. How can you help keep manatees safe?

ACTIVITIES & TOOLS

TRACK YOUR EATING AND SLEEPING

Manatees spend many hours a day eating and resting. How many hours do you spend doing these things?

What You Need:

- notebook or calendar
- pen or pencil

❶ **For one week, keep track of when you eat and how long it takes you to eat. Write it in your notebook or on a calendar.**

❷ **Also write down when you go to bed and when you wake up. Keep track of naps, too.**

❸ **At the end of each day, add up how many hours you spent eating. Add up how many hours you spent sleeping or resting. Have an adult help you.**

❹ **Look closely at the number of hours you spent eating and sleeping each day. Do you notice any patterns? How do your patterns compare to a manatee's?**

GLOSSARY

algae: Small plants without roots or stems that grow mainly in water.

blubber: A thick layer of fat under the skin of some ocean animals.

calf: A young manatee.

coast: The land next to an ocean or sea.

communicate: To share information, ideas, or feelings with another.

currents: Parts or areas of water that move continuously in a certain direction.

flexible: Able to bend or move easily.

herbivores: Animals that only eat plants.

mammals: Warm-blooded animals that give birth to live young, which drink milk from their mothers.

migrate: To travel from one place to another place during different times of the year.

pollution: Harmful materials that damage or contaminate the air, water, or soil.

predators: Animals that hunt other animals for food.

species: One of the groups into which similar animals and plants are divided.

steer: To make something move in a particular direction.

INDEX

TO LEARN MORE

Finding more information is as easy as 1, 2, 3.

❶ Go to www.factsurfer.com

❷ Enter "manatees" into the search box.

❸ Choose your book to see a list of websites.

FACT SURFER